This ELMER book belongs to:

· · · · · · · · · · · · · · · · · · · ·

**In Memory of Barbara —
with love and thanks for Chantel, Chuck and Brett**

This American edition published in 2012 for Books are Fun by Andersen Press Ltd.,
20 Vauxhall Bridge Road, London SW1V 2SA.
Text and illustrations copyright © David McKee, 1997
The rights of David McKee to be identified as the author and illustrator
of this work have been asserted by him in accordance with
the Copyright, Designs and Patents Act, 1988.
All rights reserved.
British Library Cataloguing in Publication Data available.

Color separated in Switzerland by Photolitho AG, Zürich.
Manufactured in China by C & C Offset Printing Co., Ltd.
1-C&C-6/26/12

ISBN 978 1 84939 547 2

ELMER
and the Wind

David McKee

Andersen Press

It was a very, very windy day. Elmer, the
patchwork elephant, was sheltering in a cave
with his elephant friends, some birds and cousin
Wilbur, who was playing tricks with his voice.
The elephants laughed when Wilbur made his
voice come from a hole at the back of
the cave.

"It's not a good day for flying," said a bird.
"It's a good day to be a heavy elephant," chuckled Elmer.
"An elephant can't be blown away."
"I bet even you are afraid to go out in this wind, Elmer,"
said the bird.
"Afraid?" said Elmer. "Watch this then. Come on, Wilbur."
"Come back, don't be silly," called the elephants.
But Elmer and Wilbur had already gone out into the wind.

Once they
were behind some
trees and out of sight
of the others, Elmer led the
way into another cave.
"You're up to something, Elmer," said Wilbur.
"Yes," laughed Elmer. "Make your voice come
from out there as if we were still walking away.
Sound like me sometimes."

"I get it," said Wilbur. His voice
came from the distance, sounding like Elmer –
"It's hard to move in this wind." Then like
himself – "Careful, Elmer, hold on."

The elephants heard the voices and started to worry.
Wilbur called, "Hold on to something, Elmer. Look out!"

"HELP!" came Elmer's voice. "HELP! I'm flying."
Wilbur called, "ELMER! COME BACK! ELMER! OH,
HELP! HELP!"

"Elmer's being blown away, we must help," said an elephant.
"If you go out you'll be blown away too," said a bird.
"Form a chain, trunks holding tails," said another elephant.
They crept out of the cave, each elephant holding the tail of the elephant in front.

"Look at them," said Elmer. "They
do look funny."
"Come back, you'll be blown away," called Wilbur.
The elephants all started to speak at once, but
because they were holding on with their trunks,
their voices sounded very strange:
"We've been fooled!"
"It's an Elmer and Wilbur trick."
Then they backed back into the cave
and looked funnier than ever.

When they were safely back in the cave, Elmer and
Wilbur returned as well. The elephants enjoyed the joke
but a bird said, "That was very silly, Elmer."
"But really, Bird," said Elmer, "an elephant can't be
blown away. I'll walk to those trees and back to prove it."
"Another trick," said an elephant, as Elmer walked away.

They watched as Elmer disappeared behind
some trees.

Then they heard Elmer's voice calling, "Help! I can't
keep on the ground."

The elephants laughed, "Very funny, Wilbur."

The voice came again, "HELP! I'M FLYING!"

The elephants laughed louder than ever.

"It's not me this time," said Wilbur.

"Look!" said a bird. "It isn't Wilbur."
The elephants stared: there was Elmer above the trees.
"What's he doing up there?" gasped an elephant.
"It's called flying," said a bird.
"Poor Elmer," said an elephant.

"It's my ears," thought Elmer. "They're acting as wings."
Wilbur and the others seemed very small as he flew away.

"This is really quite fun," thought Elmer after a while. He could see the other animals sheltering from the wind. They stared to see an elephant fly by.
"It's Elmer," said a lion. "I expect he's up to another of his tricks."

At last the wind dropped and Elmer landed. "Oh dear," he thought. "It's going to be a long walk home. It serves me right for being so silly."

When the wind stopped, the birds flew off to find Elmer and help guide him home. When at last the elephants saw the birds flying above the trees, they knew that Elmer was near. They rushed to meet him to hear about his adventure.

"You were wrong, Elmer," said the bird.
"An elephant can be blown away."
"You were wrong too, bird," laughed Elmer.
"It was a lovely day for flying!"

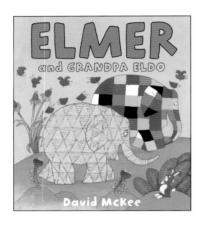

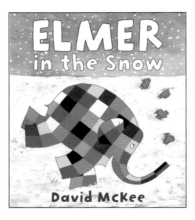

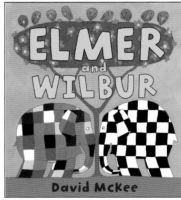

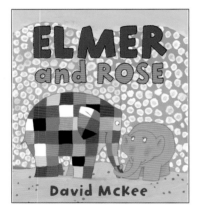

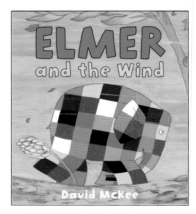

Enjoy more Elmer stories from:

www.andersenpressusa.com

www.lernerbooks.com

www.oceanhousemedia.com